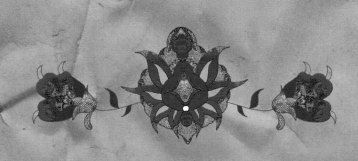

First published in Great Britain in 2009 and the USA in 2010 by
Frances Lincoln Children's Books, 4 Torriano Mews,
Torriano Avenue, London NW5 2RZ
www.franceslincoln.com

British Library Cataloguing in Publication Data
available on request

ISBN: 978-1-84507-912-3

Illustrated with watercolour, colour pencil and collage

Set in Giovanni LT Book

Printed in Dongguan, Guangdong, China by Toppan Leefung in March 2011
3 5 7 9 8 6 4 2

Pea Boy

and other stories from Iran

Retold by **Elizabeth Laird**

Illustrated by **Shirin Adl**

F
FRANCES LINCOLN
CHILDREN'S BOOKS

For Gabriel Iraj, Eleanor Nargess
and Simeon Omid Francis-Dehqani – E.L.

For my Prince Charming, Kamyar – S.A.

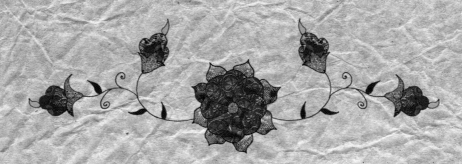

Contents

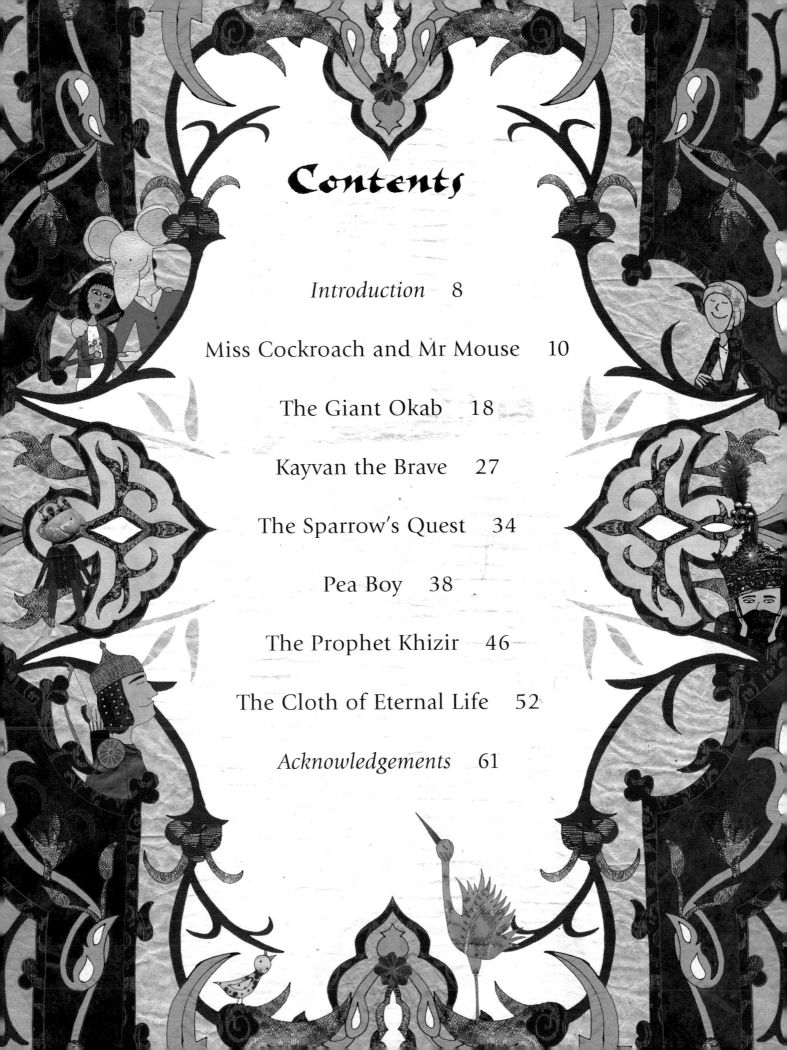

Introduction

I first went to Iran many years ago. In those days a powerful king called a Shah ruled from the Peacock Throne. He was surrounded by courtiers, and smartly-dressed soldiers guarded him. His palaces stood in beautiful gardens and his treasure-house was full of riches: ropes of pearls, diamond necklaces, rubies as big as pigeons' eggs, sapphires and emeralds spilling out of alabaster bowls, crowns and swords and goblets made of gold and encrusted with jewels.

You'll find shahs and their viziers (advisors) in many Iranian tales, including the ones in this book. There's a treasure-house in these pages, too, which dazzled the Pea Boy in the story on page 38 just as the real Shah's treasure once dazzled me.

I went back to Iran a while ago. There's no Shah in the country now, but many things remain as they were in bygone days. Mountains striped white with snow tower above Tehran, the capital city. Further north, near the Caspian Sea, there are dense forests where bears, lynxes and foxes still roam. You'll find yourself in such a forest when you read *The Cloth of Eternal Life*.

There are great deserts in Iran, too. It's hot and tiring travelling through them. The road stretches on for mile after mile, but every now and then you come to a greener place, just as Kayvan does in *Kayvan the Brave*, where trees fringe a stream or pool. There you might find an old farmhouse surrounded by high brick walls. If you're invited in, as I sometimes was, you'll be offered delicious stews and rice yellow with saffron and the most juicy peaches and apricots you can imagine.

In the cities there are still great bazaars, where shopkeepers like the Pea Boy's father sit in their crowded shops in narrow, covered lanes. These days, you can buy computer games and plastic toys and mobile phones in the bazaar, but more oldfashioned merchants still sell silks and velvets, almonds, cinnamon, saffron and rose-water.

My favourite places in Iran are the gardens where sparrows peck and flocks of pigeons wheel in flight. Spiky, dark cypress trees are reflected in pools of water and students sit between the rose-beds studying their books. It is in such a garden that poor young Mohsen stands on his wedding day when the terrifying monster bird flies down to capture him, in the story of *The Giant Okab*.

Iran is a country full of stories: of jinns and fairies and demons, faithful mice and frivolous cockroaches, foolish young weavers and curious sparrows. Nowadays there are new stories alongside the old ones. They tell of revolutionaries and soldiers, wars, and the leaders and teachers of Islam. But the people who live out these stories, those who tell them and those who listen, are the same – quick-witted, humorous, long-suffering, and generous to strangers.

Elizabeth Laird

Miss Cockroach and Mr Mouse

Miss Cockroach, who lived with her father in a crack above the window in the kitchen wall, was the prettiest young insect you ever did see, but oh, she was silly and vain! She lazed about all day long, burnishing her lustrous wings and fluttering her long antennae, and she never gave a thought to the pots that needed scouring, or the crumbs that waited to be gathered up, or the rips that had to be mended in her poor father's shirt. But Mr Cockroach loved his daughter, and never a complaint did he make.

One dreadful day, Mr Cockroach was tempted out of his home by a dribble of spilt honey, and just as he was about to start slurping it up, the cook saw him, and hurled his spoon at him. One of Mr Cockroach's back legs was broken, and he only just managed to crawl back to safety.

"I can't look after you any more, my dear," he croaked to his daughter, "and you're too silly to manage on your own. Put those good looks of yours to use at last. Rich Mr Ramazan, the merchant of Hamadan, is looking for a wife, and he'll marry you for sure."

So Miss Cockroach made a dress from a yellow onion-skin , and a cloak from the purple rind of an aubergine, and slippers from split almonds. Then she put rouge on her cheeks, lined her eyes with kohl, rubbed her lips with red raspberry juice and painted henna on her fingers and toes. When she was quite, quite beautiful she set off on the road to Hamadan.

On the way she met the grocer, and she waved her antennae at him in a very saucy way.

"Where are you off to, all dressed up like a queen?" asked the grocer.

"I'm off to Hamadan to marry Ramazan, because I'm too silly to manage on my own," replied Miss Cockroach.

"Marry me instead," said the grocer, "but if you spill my coffee, I'll beat you with my broom."

"I wouldn't like that at all," said Miss Cockroach, and she went on her way.

Next she met the butcher, and she smiled at him with her raspberry-red lips.

"Where are you going in your pretty onion-skin dress?" asked the butcher.

"I'm off to Hamadan to marry Ramazan, because I'm too silly to manage on my own," replied Miss Cockroach.

"Marry me instead," said the butcher, "but if you burn my dinner, I'll beat you with a chicken bone."

"I wouldn't like that at all," said Miss Cockroach, and she went on her way.

Soon she met a blacksmith, and she pirouetted past him in her almond slippers.

"Where are you off to, as lovely as a bride on her wedding day?" asked the blacksmith.

"I'm off to Hamadan to marry Ramazan, because I'm too silly to manage on my own," replied Miss Cockroach.

"Marry me instead," said the blacksmith, "but if you break my tea glass, I'll beat you with my fire tongs."

"I wouldn't like that at all," said Miss Cockroach, and she went on her way.

Soon she met Mr Mouse. He was sitting outside his house wearing silver trousers and a cap of woven gold thread.

"Oh, oh! You beautiful creature!" he cried. "And where are you going in your gorgeous aubergine cloak and delicate almond slippers?"

"I'm off to Hamadan to marry Ramazan, because I'm too silly to manage on my own," replied Miss Cockroach.

"Marry me instead," said Mr Mouse. "I'll feed you on honey and tell you stories, and I'll never beat you, whatever you do, but only tickle you under your chin."

"I'd like that very much," said Miss Cockroach, "and I'll marry you as soon as you like."

And so the wedding was arranged. All the cockroaches came in their best clothes, and the mice wore splendid uniforms with buttons made of scarlet berries.

Miss Cockroach loved her husband dearly, but she was the silliest wife that ever lived. She spilled his coffee and burnt his dinner and broke all his tea glasses one by one, and though she tried her best, poor Mr Mouse's house was never properly swept, and his breakfast was never ready, and the holes in his socks grew larger and larger. But he loved his little cockroach and every morning, before he went off to work at the Shah's palace to collect the crumbs that fell from the royal table, he never forgot to tickle her under the chin.

One fine morning, Miss Cockroach decided to wash her husband's shiny silver trousers, so off she went to the stream. She dipped the trousers into the water and scrubbed and soaked and rinsed, leaning further and further down the bank. But the stream was flowing fast, and the trousers were heavy with water. Suddenly they slipped from her hands and floated away, their silvery threads glinting in the sunlight.

"Oh, oh! Come back, you stupid things!" shouted Miss Cockroach, bending forward even further. "Oh, oh! I'm falling in!"

And she might have fallen in and been swept away, but just in time, she managed to catch hold of a reed.

Now poor Miss Cockroach was in trouble, for the reed was only a thin little thing, and it swayed backwards and forwards, bending right down until it nearly touched the water. Miss Cockroach could only cling on to it for dear life, calling out in a faint voice, "Help me! Save me! Oh Mr Mouse, my husband dear! Where are you? Come and save your wife!"

Now, at that very moment a troop of the Shah's soldiers trotted by. They laughed at the sight of the tiny cockroach in her onion-skin gown and almond slippers wobbling about on her reed, but they had no time to stop and help her.

"And what did you see on your rounds this morning?" the Shah asked the captain, when he returned with his men to the palace.

"Nothing, sire," he answered, "except for a silly little cockroach in an onion-skin dress who was clinging to a reed in the stream, calling on a mouse to save her."

Just at that moment, Mr Mouse was scurrying past on his way to tidy up the crumbs in the dining-room, and he heard what the captain was saying.

"My wife! My poor little cockroach!" he squeaked. "What is she up to this time?" And he ran to the stream as fast as his legs would carry him.

Miss Cockroach, who by this time was more dead than alive, still clung to the reed with her eyes tight shut, moaning softly, "Mouse! Mr Mouse! Save me!"

"Oh my little wife, my pearl of beauty!" cried Mr Mouse. "Give me your hand and I'll pull you to safety!"

"My hand?" wailed Miss Cockroach. "But if I let go of this reed, I'll fall straight into the water."

"Then give me a foot, oh star of perfection!"

"A foot?" screeched Miss Cockroach. "There's cramp in all my feet and I can't move any of them."

"Then I'll catch you by the hair."

"No no! I spent a whole hour combing it this morning. You'll tangle it all up again."

Mr Mouse jumped up and down, beside himself with anxiety.

"What can I do, O light of my eyes, if you won't let me save you?"

"Bring me a ladder, a golden one," commanded Miss Cockroach, "and hurry, before I drown!"

Mr Mouse ran up and down the bank, muttering to himself, "A ladder! Now where can I find a ladder? And a golden one at that?"

Just as he was about to give his wife up for lost, he spied the feathery tops of carrots growing in a nearby field. He ran to them and with all his strength pulled up the biggest he could see. Then he set to work, gnawing and nibbling, and a minute later the carrot had turned into a golden ladder with neat little steps running all the way to the top.

Mr Mouse rushed back to the stream.

"Here, my love, here's your golden ladder," he panted. He laid it across the water to Miss Cockroach's reed, and she flicked her hair back and minced daintily down it, holding up the skirt of her onion-skin dress.

As soon as she reached the bank, Mr Mouse caught her in his arms, and what with the excitement and the relief, Miss Cockroach fainted dead away.

Faithful Mr Mouse picked her up in his arms and carried her home to his house, taking care not to let her aubergine cloak trail in the mud.

The next morning, Miss Cockroach sneezed three times before breakfast, and her little body ached all over.

"You've caught a cold," Mr Mouse said anxiously, "and there's only one cure for that: turnip soup, well cooked with onions, and as hot as can be."

So Mr Mouse scampered off to the fields, and pulled up a turnip and a pair of onions, and he dragged them all the way to the Shah's kitchen, where a pot of water was boiling on the fire. He peeled and chopped and dropped everything into the pot, and when he thought the soup was well and truly cooked, he climbed up the side of the pot to look. But the pot was hot, and his little feet began to burn, and he had to hop about on the rim. And the steam went into his eyes and he lost his balance, and down he fell, right into the boiling soup!

Miss Cockroach waited and waited, lying on her bed, snuffling and coughing with her cold. But her dear husband, her Mr Mouse, would never come home again, for he was boiled up with the soup.

When she learned what had happened, Miss Cockroach cried until she thought her heart would break.

"Oh, oh! My dear Mr Mouse! You were the only one who loved me and forgave me all my silliness!"

And Miss Cockroach took off her onion-skin dress and her purple cloak and her almond slippers. She washed the raspberry juice off her lips and the kohl from around her eyes, and cut off her long hair.

"I'll never marry anyone again," she said, "and I won't be silly any more. I'll behave like a sensible cockroach, and I won't pretend to be anything else."

Miss Cockroach learned her lesson, and from that day onwards she always wore black, and learned to work hard and be sensible and live simply, with her father, in the crack in the kitchen wall. And that is why you will never see a cockroach wearing an aubergine cloak with almond slippers, and you'll never find a silly one, either.

The Giant Okab

There was once a young Persian silk spinner called Yusof, whose mind spun dreams while his fingers spun the soft silk threads.

"I'm not going to sit here for ever doing this dull work," he told himself. "One day I'm going to see the world."

Carefully, he saved all the money he earned and put it away in a leather bag. When the bag was heavy with the weight of gold, he said goodbye to his father and mother and off he sailed to Arabia.

As soon as the ship docked, Yusof jumped ashore and began to explore the town, admiring mosques and palaces, peering down interesting alleyways and listening to strange music from behind closed doors. Quickly he found himself a room in a pilgrim's hostel, and was soon sitting in the inner courtyard with a cool drink in his hand and the chatter of other travellers all around him.

But suddenly, just as it was time to look for some dinner, a violent wind sent the dust whirling round in furious eddies, the trees of the courtyard flailed about as if a hurricane had struck, and everything went dark.

The khan's owner dashed out of his kitchen.

"Run, sirs! Run for shelter!" he shouted. "The Giant Okab is coming!"

Everyone scattered to hide in their rooms, but Yusof had left his bag of money on the far side of the courtyard, so he darted across to fetch it.

Before he knew what was happening, a vast bird swooped down out of the sky. Its beak was made of brass and was as long as five men laid end to end, and its wings were the size of a ship's sails.

Its iron claws were as sharp as spears, while its feathers were made of hard, glittering copper.

One swish of the creature's wings sent Yusof tumbling to the ground, and a second later the Giant Okab had snatched him up in its claws, which cut deep into Yusof's flesh so that he cried out in agony.

"Put me down!" he managed to shout. "Aah! Stop!"

The Giant Okab snapped its brass beak, making a hideous clanging sound.

"You coward," it screeched, in a voice that grated like metal dragged over rocks. "Accept your fate like a man. Tonight is the twelfth full moon of the year, and you are the sacrifice I must take to the Land of the Demons."

"Take someone else. Don't take me!" pleaded Yusof.

"Who? Who shall I take?" thundered the Giant Okab.

Yusof couldn't think of anyone. He didn't know a soul in this strange land.

"Please," was all he could answer. "I'm young, and my whole life is before me. Let me go."

The Giant Okab hovered for a moment with Yusof in its grasp.

"I'll let you go," it said, "if you promise to give me your son on the day of his wedding."

Yusof wasn't married, and he had no children, so this was an easy thing to promise. "My son?" he said, almost laughing with relief. "Oh yes, you can have my son!"

The Giant Okab dropped him as if he had been a sack of corn, and Yusof, bruised and bleeding, thanked God for his lucky escape.

Yusof travelled on for a year and day, seeing enough wonders to satisfy all his dreams. Then, homesick at last, he returned to Persia. He took up his old trade of silk-spinning, did well, and married a beautiful girl. A year later they had a son and called him Mohsen, and the following year a daughter called Zohreh was born.

Mohsen was a happy little boy. Everyone liked him. He played with the merchants' sons in the town and with his friend the shepherd's daughter in the desert, while Zohreh his sister grew up as pretty as a rose. Their father Yusof prospered and the family lived in great comfort.

When Mohsen was twenty, his father and mother arranged a marriage for him with the daughter of a rich merchant.

"When shall we have the wedding?" Yusof's wife asked him.

"Whenever you like," said Yusof.

"The day of the twelfth full moon, I think," said Yusof's wife, happily looking forward to the wonderful dishes she would cook for the wedding feast.

Yusof wasn't listening. He was calculating in his head how much the wedding would cost. He had quite forgotten the Giant Okab and the promise he had made.

Mohsen's wedding day came. The house was filled with laughter and excitement as guests crowded into the garden. The merchant's daughter arrived in her bridal gown and veil, and though she looked proud and spoilt, Mohsen was excited and happy in his silk and velvet wedding suit.

The musicians struck up their songs. The feast began.

Then, all of a sudden, a wild wind sent the dust whirling upwards in huge spirals, the trees in the courtyard tossed violently about, and everything went dark.

As the guests looked up into the sky, a vast bird swooped down. Its huge brass beak snapped with a hideous jangle, and the beat of its gigantic wings was like the clatter of heavy chains. Its copper feathers grated as its claws reached out to strike. Everyone shrieked, but the loudest scream of all came from the bride.

"The Giant Okab! It's the Giant Okab! Whatever did you do to offend it, you fool?" she yelled at Mohsen. "I'll never marry you now!"

And she pushed through the crowd and ran away.

Yusof suddenly remembered the promise he'd made many years before. Frozen with horror, he watched as the Giant Okab seized poor Mohsen in its claws.

The young man's screams of terror brought him back to life and he dashed forwards and threw himself on the ground.

"Take me!" he shouted. "Sacrifice me to the Demons, only let my son go!"

The Giant Okab tossed Mohsen aside, and a second later its fearsome claws were drawing streams of blood from Yusof's chest.

But Yusof's wife could not bear to hear her husband's shout of pain.

"Let him go! Take me!" she called out.

The Giant Okab dropped Yusof and sank its claws into her shoulders, and she gasped and cried out in agony.

Then, before anyone could stop her, Mohsen's sister Zohreh ran forwards and begged to be taken instead of her mother, but when she too screamed with the pain of the great claws ripping through her skin, the Giant Okab let her go.

Mohsen by now had picked himself up and summoned all his courage.

"You came for me, and I'll go with you," he said bravely, but before the Giant Okab could seize him, a ragged young girl threw herself right into the huge bird's claws. Though pale with fear, she never uttered a sound as the Giant Okab's talons gripped her, and a second later the wind whipped through the courtyard again as the bird's great wings beat and it lifted its victim up into the sky.

"Who was that girl?" the wedding guests asked each other, looking up into the sky in pity and admiration as the Giant Okab disappeared with the girl held in his talons.

"Look! It's coming back!" someone shouted, and the guests began to run about, desperately looking for somewhere to hide. Only Mohsen and Zohreh had the courage to watch and wait.

To their amazement, there was no roaring wind this time. The Giant Okab floated slowly down to earth and set the girl down gently. She lay still and pale, but her eyes were open, and though she was bleeding from her many wounds, not one sound came from her, not even the slightest whimper of pain.

Mohsen and Zohreh ran over to her.

"Don't I know you?" Zohreh began. "Aren't you...?"

But Mohsen was staring at the giant bird. He grabbed his sister's arm. "Look!" he cried.

An unearthly light was filling the courtyard and the three of them watched in astonishment as the Giant Okab's copper feathers melted into each other, and its wings grew transparent and disappeared.

The brass beak shimmered and shrank until it was no larger than a bowl. The claws fused together and became a shining sword.

A moment later, a handsome young warrior, dressed as a knight in chainmail with a brass helmet on his head, stood before them.

He knelt beside the ragged girl.

"You have saved me from an evil curse," he told her.

She looked up at the knight, and as she smiled, Mohsen saw that in spite of her old, ragged clothes she was the most beautiful girl he had ever seen.

"What curse?" she asked the knight.

"When I was a child, I killed a sparrow," he answered, "and the King of the Birds laid this terrible spell on me. Every year, on the night of the twelfth moon, I have had to take a sacrifice to the Land of the Demons. The only person who could break the spell was a human being who would bear pain and had no fear of death."

"But why did you let yourself be taken?" said Mohsen, lifting the girl to her feet. "Why did you want to save me?"

"Don't you recognise me?" she answered. "I'm your childhood friend, the shepherd girl. I loved you when we were children and we played together in the desert, and I love you still. I didn't mind dying for you."

Mohsen's parents and all the wedding guests had come hurrying out of their hiding places.

"What's happened?" they were asking. "Tell us!"

So Mohsen told them everything. Then he took the shepherd girl's hand and said, "This is my wedding day, but the girl you chose for me has run away. I've found a bride worthier than her, one who truly loves me, and I'll love her for the rest of my life."

So Mohsen married the shepherd girl. They lived happily ever after, and there was always plenty of butter on their bread.

Kayvan the Brave

A long time ago there was a weaver's apprentice called Kayvan. He was a big lad with broad shoulders and long legs, who knew nothing of the great wide world beyond the weaving shop and the little house he shared with his mother. He sat all day and worked at his loom, and in the evening he went home, ate the supper his mother had cooked and went to bed.

One day, as he worked away, throwing his shuttle to and fro, he caught sight of two mice nibbling at the cloth he was making. He was so startled that the shuttle shot out of his hand, flew through the air and hit both the mice at once, killing them on the spot.

The other apprentices, who liked to tease Kayvan, began to stamp and cheer.

"Wa-hey!" they cried. "Did you see that? What a warrior! What a man!"

And they began to chant:

"Kayvan the brave
with his arrow and bow
killed two lions
with only one blow."

Kayvan, who believed everything he was told, blushed with pleasure and pride.

"You're in the wrong job, my son," one of the apprentices said, winking at the others. "An archer, that's what you should be. Out hunting. In the desert. A talent like yours is wasted here."

"Really? Do you really think so?" Kayvan said .

"A hunter! Of course! Yes, yes!" the others chorused, laughing behind their hands.

Their words lit a fire in Kayvan's heart. He stood up and left the weaving shop, not even stopping to lift his jacket from its hook, and ran straight to the bazaar. There he bought himself a bow and a set of arrows.

The bow was a good one, fine and strong, and the arrows were straight and sharp, but Kayvan frowned. Something was missing. At last he realised what it was.

"I want you to write on this," he said, handing the bow back to the shopkeeper.

"Write? What?" said the man, surprised.

Kayvan squared his shoulders and said proudly:

> *"Kayvan the brave*
> *with his arrow and bow*
> *killed two lions*
> *with only one blow."*

The shopkeeper stared at him respectfully.

"Two lions, eh? Yes, sir. At once, sir!"

When the work was done, Kayvan hitched the bow over his shoulder and marched off into the desert to look for game. On and on he went until, tired and thirsty, he saw a stream with a tree bending over it. He stopped and took a long, cool drink.

It was shady and pleasant by the stream.

"Even a great hunter needs to rest now and then," he told himself, and he hung his bow and arrows in the tree, lay down and fell asleep.

A little while later, a captain of the Shah's cavalry came trotting by. He stopped to look at Kayvan, then saw the bow and arrows in the tree.

"What's a strong young fellow like this doing all on his own out here?" he asked himself. "And what's that written on his bow?" He leaned forward to read the inscription. "Two lions with one blow, eh? Well, well!"

He got off his horse and sat down beside Kayvan, who woke with a start and stared at him. "Now, my boy, who are you?" the captain barked.

Kayvan opened his eyes and blinked. He couldn't remember where he was.

"Kayvan the brave

with his arrow and bow... " he began feebly.

"Yes, yes. I've read all that. But what are you doing here?" demanded the captain.

"I – I came to hunt," said Kayvan, sitting up.

"I see. Good shot, I suppose? Range, accuracy, distance and so on and so forth?"

"Oh, yes," said Kayvan proudly, remembering the mice.

"Excellent!" cried the captain. "You're just the sort of chap we need in the army. You'd like to fight for your Shah and country, eh? Honour and glory, victory or death, and so on?"

"Fight?" said Kayvan, puzzled. "Glory? Is there a war?"

"Unfortunately not, but there's bound to be one soon," the captain said, mounting his horse. "Follow me!"

And so Kayvan joined the army and lived comfortably at the Shah's expense, eating as much as he liked and marching about in his uniform. He never said much, but always looked grand and brave.

"He's a great champion, you know," everyone whispered. "Killed three – or was it four? – lions with only one arrow."

Soon enough, a war broke out, just as the captain had predicted. He came to find Kayvan, cracking his riding whip.

"Here's your chance to show what you're made of, my boy. Been champing at the bit, I'm sure. There'll be no holding you now!"

"Eh?" said Kayvan.

"Get yourself off to the stables. The grooms have saddled a horse for you. Then off you go to the battlefield!"

Kayvan had never ridden a horse before. At the stables, he stared in dismay at the huge war horse the grooms led out to him.

"I'll never be able to stay on this thing," he thought, so he said to the grooms, "Do me a favour, boys. Tie my feet together underneath its belly."

The grooms hurried to obey.

"He's got some wonderful trick up his sleeve, you'll see," they whispered.

From far away came the sound of the enemy's trumpets. The war horse knew what their wild music meant. He loved fighting. He pawed at the ground, flattened his ears and shot out of the stable. Kayvan nearly lost hold of the reins, and had to clutch at the horse's mane.

"Help! Stop!" he shouted, dropping his bow and arrows, but the horse only bolted faster, striking sparks from the stones with his great iron hooves, leaping over streams, bounding over bushes and dodging between trees as the sound of the enemy's drums and trumpets grew louder and louder.

In desperation, Kayvan clutched at a passing branch, expecting the horse to skid to a halt, but the horse was going so fast that the tree was torn up by its roots. On and on they raced, with Kayvan and the tree tangled up together on the horse's back.

The enemy was in sight now. Their lines of spears and helmets glinted in the sun. But Kayvan, the tree and the horse galloped straight towards them, and it was a sight so terrifying that strong men trembled like babies.

"I can't stop! He's run away!" Kayvan was shouting.

The enemy soldiers turned to each other, their faces pale with fear.

"What's that he's saying? *Don't stop? Come this way?* There's a whole army behind him! There must be! He's calling them to follow him, and if they're all like this great champion, who can tear a tree up by its roots, we haven't got a chance!"

And they turned and fled, every man of them, and the Shah's soldiers raced after them, hassling and harrying them all the way home.

The Shah was so pleased with Kayvan that he presented him with golden dishes and fine robes and jewels and palaces and gardens full of pomegranate trees, and he made him Commander-in-Chief of all his armies.

But Kayvan, who had seen enough of war, never wanted to fight again. He kept his armies safe at home and for as long as he lived, the whole country enjoyed days of peace and plenty.

The Sparrow's Quest

A hungry sparrow, one cold winter's day, fluttered about hunting for something to eat. At last she saw a movement on an icy pond.

Aha! she thought. A grub! and down she swooped, hoping for a meal.

But there was no grub, only a twig blowing in the breeze.

The ice was so cold that the sparrow's feet began to sting.

"Oh, cruel ice!" she exclaimed. "Nothing has ever hurt me as much as this. There's no one else like you, who can give a poor little bird such pain. How does it feel to be the greatest power there is?"

The ice creaked and cracked as a laugh shivered along his bright surface.

"Powerful? Me?" he growled. "How wrong you are. The sun is much stronger than I am. When the spring comes, he'll shine his hot rays down on me and I'll splinter and melt away. You must ask the sun how it feels to be powerful, little bird."

The sparrow, glad to lift her feet from the ice's freezing surface, flew up and up into the sky, as close to the sun as she dared.

"Tell me, great sun," she chirped, shielding her face with a wing from the sun's blinding rays, "are you the greatest power there is? I thought it was the ice, but he tells me you'll melt him away when the spring comes."

Flames shot out from the sun's fiery heart, threatening to singe the sparrow's feathers.

"The greatest power on earth?" he roared. "It's not me, no no, not me. How could it be, since the clouds can cover me and hide me from below?

Ask the clouds, sparrow. Ask the clouds."

The sparrow flew on, seeking refuge from the sun's tremendous heat in the wet mistiness of the clouds.

"Cool wet clouds, mighty storm clouds, are you greater than the sun?" she asked. "For that's what he tells me."

Lightning flickered and thunder groaned all around, making the sparrow's feathers shiver.

"Powerful? Not us," rumbled the clouds. "The wind can blow us anywhere it chooses. Go and ask the wind."

The wind picked up the sparrow and tumbled her about in its gusts and eddies until she hardly knew where she was.

"Stop, wind! Is it true what the clouds have told me, that you are the greatest power there is?" shouted the sparrow.

The wind snatched up flurries of leaves from the ground below and played with them as it answered, "Little sparrow, how can that be? There is something I can never move, however hard I blow. The mountain is more powerful than me. Go to the mountain and ask him."

The sparrow flew to the mountain, and perched on the very top.

"Mountain, can you hear me?" she sang out. "The wind tells me that you are more powerful even than him. Are you the greatest thing on earth?"

Deep inside the mountain, rocks clashed and ground together, before at last the mountain spoke.

"Look around you, little bird. Grass covers me from my feet to the crown of my head, and there's nothing I can do to shake it off. Ask the grass who is most powerful here."

So the sparrow, looking down at the grass, called out, "Grass, grass, did you hear the mountain? Are you the most powerful thing there is?"

The blades of grass all around her shook and rattled as a thousand voices called out in reedy tones, "Oh sparrow, how can you think we are powerful, when worms can burrow through us and disturb our roots?"

The sparrow, who was very tired by now, and faint with hunger, looked around until she saw a worm hole. She stood above it and called down, "Worm, are you there? The grass tells me how powerful you are – the most powerful thing on earth. Tell me, is it true?"

The humble worm had never been asked such a question before. Unwisely, he poked his head out of his hole, and sighed, "Oh, how I wish I was! Then I would never be afraid of being eaten by a hungry sparrow."

Too late, he saw who it was who had called down to him, for at that moment the sparrow opened her beak and began to gobble him up.

Just before he disappeared altogether, the worm managed to gasp, "How does it feel then, cruel sparrow, to be the greatest thing on earth?"

The sparrow swallowed, and wiped her beak on the grass.

"A little less hungry," she said.

Pea Boy

A poor shopkeeper was setting out for work one morning, and he said to his wife, "I fancy soup for my dinner today, my dear. Why don't you make it nice and hot, and send someone down to the shop with it?"

So his wife sliced up vegetables and chopped up meat, and dropped them into her cooking pot with a handful of rice and some chickpeas and pickles for flavour. When the soup was cooked, she poured some into a bowl and said with a sigh and a tear, "Oh, how I wish I had a little son who could run down to the shop with his father's dinner!"

At that very moment, a chickpea hopped out of the cooking pot.

"Don't cry, Mother," he said. "I'm your son, and I'll take the soup to my father."

Then he picked up the bowl of soup, balanced it on his head and off he ran to the shop.

The shopkeeper opened his eyes wide when he saw a chickpea with a bowl of soup on his head.

"Who are you?" he demanded.

"I'm your son, and I've brought you your dinner," said Pea Boy.

"That's all very well," said the shopkeeper, taking the soup, "but if you were a good son, you'd go to the palace and make that rascally Shah pay me the penny he's owed me these many long years."

"Right away, Father," said Pea Boy, and off he ran towards the palace.

On the way, he came to a stream where an old woman was washing her clothes.

"Please, old woman, will you wash my cap for me?" he asked.

"Certainly not," said the old woman. "You can wash it yourself."

"Then I'll drink up all the water in the stream," said Pea Boy, and he bent down and drank and drank until not a drop was left.

A little further on he met a leopard.

"Where are you going, Pea Boy?" asked the leopard.

"I'm off to get my father's penny from the Shah," said Pea Boy.

"Then I'll come with you," said the leopard.

But Pea Boy ran so fast that soon the leopard was worn out.

"I can't go any further," he gasped.

"Hop inside my mouth, then," said Pea Boy. "I'll carry you."

And he opened his mouth wide, and the leopard jumped in, and on they went to the palace.

Next they met a wolf.

"Where are you going, Pea Boy?" asked the wolf.

"I'm going to ask the Shah for my father's penny," said Pea Boy.

"Then I'll come with you," said the wolf.

But they hadn't gone more than a mile or two when the wolf cried out, "You're too fast for me, Pea Boy. I'm all hot and sweaty."

"Hop inside my mouth then," said Pea Boy, "and I'll carry you."

And he opened his mouth wide, wide, and the wolf jumped in, and on they went to the palace.

A little further on they met a jackal.

"Where are you going, Pea Boy?" asked the jackal.

"I'm going to the palace to get my father's penny from the Shah," said Pea Boy.

"Then I'll come with you," said the jackal.

But the jackal wasn't nearly fast enough for Pea Boy.

"I can't keep up with you," he panted. "My feet hurt."

"Hop inside my mouth, then," said Pea Boy. "I'll carry you."

And he opened his mouth wide, wide, wide, and the jackal jumped in, and on and on they ran.

When they arrived at the palace, Pea Boy called out, "I've come to get my father's penny from the Shah!"

He made such a noise that the Shah himself came out.

"Who dares speak to me like that?" he said, with a ferocious scowl, and he called his servants and said, "Take this insolent pea and throw him to the fighting cocks!"

So the Shah's servants took Pea Boy, threw him to the fighting cocks, and locked him in for the night.

Now the fighting cocks were fearsome birds, with long, sharp beaks and vicious claws, but as soon as he was alone with them, Pea Boy opened his mouth and shouted, "Jackal, come out and kill these cocks for me!"

Out leapt the jackal, and a minute later all the fighting cocks were dead. Then the jackal jumped out of the window and ran away home.

The next morning, when the Shah's servants came to look, they found the fighting cocks dead and Pea Boy alive and well.

When the Shah heard the news, he roared, "Take this naughty vegetable and throw him to the horses!"

So Pea Boy was carried off to the stables and locked in for the night with the horses.

When all the servants had gone, Pea Boy cried out, "Wolf! Come out and eat the horses!"

Out jumped the wolf, and went *snip snap* with his jaws and ate up all the horses, until there wasn't a hoof or an ear or a tail left behind. Then the wolf wriggled out under the door and ran away home.

In the morning, the Shah's servants found that all the horses had disappeared, and Pea Boy was sleeping peacefully in the straw.

The Shah was furious when he heard what had happened.

"My lions will deal with this wicked morsel!" he bellowed.

So Pea Boy was thrown to the lions.

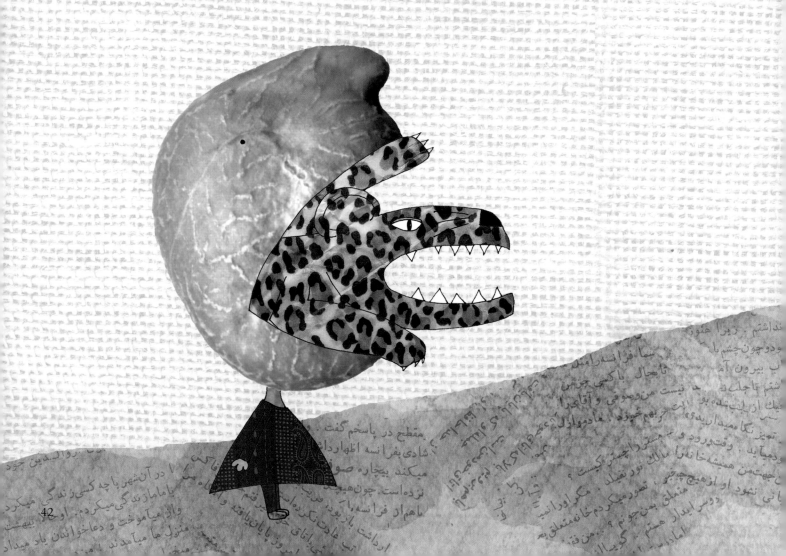

The lions circled round him hungrily, but Pea Boy called out, "Leopard! Come out and kill the lions!"

At once, the leopard jumped out of his mouth and slashed with his claws and bit with his teeth until all the lions were torn into little tiny pieces. Then off he ran to his own home.

The next morning, the Shah's servants found Pea Boy scratching his head with a lion's whisker, and when they told the Shah, he stamped up and down in such a temper that the pillars of the palace shook.

"Fill a room with straw, and set it alight, and throw this horrible creature into it so that he'll be burned up and leave me in peace," he yelled.

So the Shah's servants filled a room with straw, and set light to it, and threw Pea Boy right into its burning heart. But Pea Boy opened his mouth and all the water of the stream shot out and doused the fire with a sizzle and a hiss.

41

The Shah's servants hardly dared to tell him that Pea Boy had escaped again. But to their surprise, the Shah's anger had burned out like the fire. He just put his head in his hands and wondered what to do.

"Send for my old vizier," he said at last. "He'll know how to kill this monster."

Now the vizier was a wise old man, and when he had heard the sorry tale, he said to the Shah, "You'll never get the better of that cheeky pea. Send him to the treasure-house to find his father's penny, and let him take what he wants. Then perhaps he'll leave you in peace."

So Pea Boy was taken to the treasure-house, and he ferreted around among the piles and piles of treasure, half-dazzled by its brilliance, until he found his father's penny.

"The Shah should pay me well for the trouble he's given me and my poor father too," he said to himself, so he opened his mouth wide, wide, wide, wide, and scooped up gold and jewels and a lot else besides, but there was so much in the treasure-house that no one could tell the difference.

Pea Boy ran all the way back to his father's shop, and gave him his penny. Then home he ran to his mother.

"Hang me upside down, Mother dear," he said, "and beat me with your spindle. Gently, mind."

So his mother hung Pea Boy upside down, and beat him very gently with her spindle, and out of his mouth poured the wondrous riches of the Shah's treasure-house.

And the shopkeeper and his wife and Pea Boy their son lived in comfort and happiness for the rest of their lives.

The Prophet Khizir

There was once a great Shah who was rich and powerful, but he lived for only one thing.

"All my life," he told his courtiers, "I have heard tales of the wonderful Prophet Khizir, who drank the water of life thousands of years ago, and lives for ever. If only I could see him once before I die!"

"But, sire," his courtiers answered, "no one can summon the Prophet Khizir. He appears when he wants to those who need him, and comes and goes as he likes."

"I will summon him!" cried the Shah. "Send out a proclamation. If anyone can show me the Prophet Khizir, he shall have his heart's desire."

Now, near the Shah's palace lived a very poor man. Hunger and sickness had worn him down, and he wept to see the pale faces of his starving children.

When he heard the Shah's proclamation, he screwed up all his courage and ran to the palace.

"I'll show you the Prophet Khizir!" he burst out, when he had been ushered into the Shah's presence. "Give me a thousand dinars, and I promise you he will appear."

"Are you sure?" the Shah asked, frowning.

"Yes, yes," the poor man cried desperately, thinking only of the food that a thousand dinars would buy, and the smiles on the faces of his children when he set a feast before them.

"Very well," said the Shah, "but if after forty days the Prophet Khizir has not appeared, your head shall be struck from your shoulders."

The poor man turned pale, but he said to himself, "What difference does it make? If I don't have the money, we'll all die of hunger before tomorrow morning. At least I'll live for forty more days, and when I'm gone, there'll be enough for my family to live on."

So he bowed his head and agreed. Taking the money, he hurried to the bazaar, and returned home laden with food.

For the next few weeks the poor man's children ate until their buttons burst, and their mother sang as she stitched them back on again. But the poor man's heart grew heavier with each day that passed.

When the forty days were over, he drew his family round him and told them about the bargain he'd made with the Shah.

"I'm going to die today," he said, "but you at least can live in comfort now. Goodbye, my darlings." They clung to him, weeping, but he tore himself away and went to the palace.

"Well?" the Shah demanded, when the poor man knelt before him. "And have you brought the Prophet Khizir?"

The poor man struck his head on the marble step in front of the Shah's throne.

"No, sire," he said. "My wife and children were starving to death and I took this chance to feed them. I'm here for my punishment. I'm ready for you to cut off my head."

The Shah looked round at his room full of courtiers, but he didn't notice the old man in the green cloak who had slipped in behind them. He summoned his first vizier.

"Tell me," he said. "What should we do to this man?"

"Honour your bargain," said the first vizier. "This rascal deceived you. Cut off his head with a great pair of scissors."

The old man in the green cloak called out, "A fool speaks folly, and only the wise speak wisdom!"

"What's your opinion?" the Shah asked the second vizier.

"Scissors are too good for this rascal," he said. "Put him in an oven and bake him till he's cooked."

"A man shows his true self only when he speaks!" the old man called out.

"And you? What do you say?" the Shah asked the third vizier.

"Why dirty an oven with the likes of him?" said the third vizier. "Cut him up with a razor into little pieces. No one will ever dare to deceive you in this way again."

"He shows his true self!" the old man sang out again.

The fourth vizier didn't wait to be asked for his opinion.

"Sire," he said. "This poor man is prepared to give his own life for the sake of his family. It's poverty, not wickedness that forced him to deceive you. Let him keep the thousand dinars, and give him a thousand more."

Before the old man in the green cloak had a chance to call out again, the Shah beckoned him forward.

"You've been quick to speak," he said, "so what do you say now?"

"I say," the old man answered, "that your first vizier is nothing but a jumped-up tailor who bought his way into your service. That's why he thinks of scissors.

"The second was a baker, who cheated his customers. What does he know of justice?

"The third was a barber, who understands only the cut of a razor.

"But the fourth vizier served your father and grandfather before you, and he speaks wisely.

This poor man made his bargain with you to save his family, and he has kept his side of it, because he has shown you the Prophet Khizir."

Then, in front of everyone's astonished eyes, the old man in the green cloak disappeared.

"The Prophet Khizir! It was the Prophet Khizir himself!" cried the Shah. "Why didn't I catch hold of him while he was here?"

He gave the poor man riches beyond his dreams, and sent his foolish advisors away. From then on, he listened only to his father's wise vizier, and ruled justly and generously.

As for the poor man, he was poor no longer, and for the rest of their lives he and his happy children blessed the name of the Prophet Khizir.

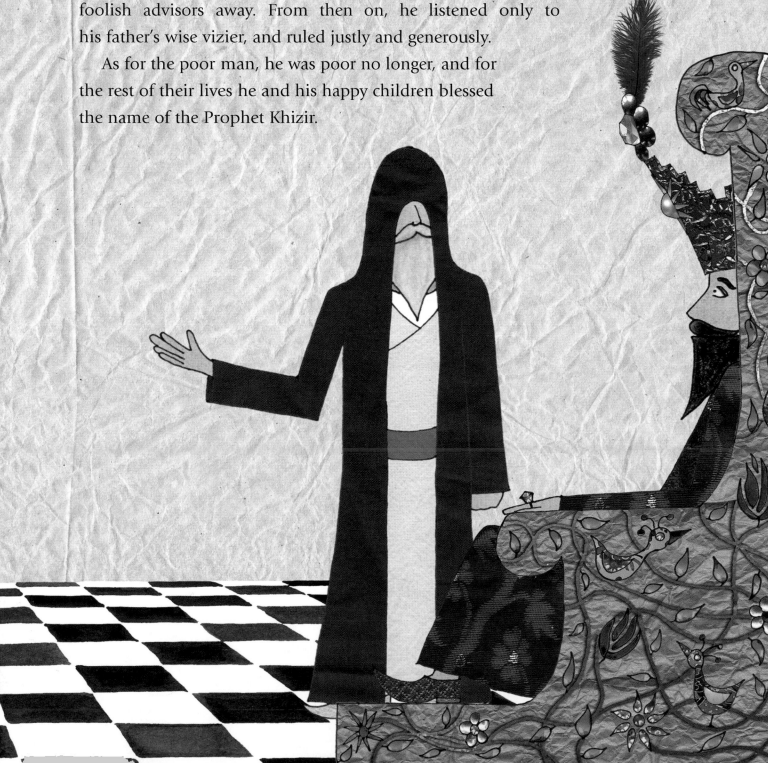

The Cloth of Eternal Life

A merchant and his son, who was a clever lad, lived alone together. They had everything that money could buy, but the old man was never happy.

"My hair's grey and my teeth are falling out," he kept grumbling. "I've got one foot in the grave already."

"No, no, Father," his son would yawn. "You'll live for years and years."

"That's all you know! Soon I'll be dead and gone, and you'll be married, with a row of dear little children, and I'll never even have the chance to bounce them on my knee."

But by then his son couldn't hear him, for he was fast asleep.

One night, a stranger knocked at their door. The merchant invited him in, and the three of them sat and ate together.

"You're a well-travelled man, by the look of you," the merchant said, noticing the stranger's worn shoes and dusty clothes.

The man nodded.

"My journeys have taken me far and wide, and I've just returned from the strangest one of all. I was passing through a deep forest, far from here. I thought I'd lost my way, but then I saw a bird with long golden feathers

which shone as brightly as the sun. I followed it, and came to a cottage."

His hosts leaned closer.

"I looked in through the window and saw an old woman. She was working at a loom, weaving her own long white hair into a cloth. Every time she pulled a hair from her head, another one grew in its place.

"I was so curious that I knocked at the cottage door and asked her what she was doing. And when she looked up at me, I saw that she wasn't old at all, in spite of her white hair, but young and beautiful. And she wasn't a woman, but a fairy.

" 'If anyone makes a garment out of this cloth, and wears it,' she told me, 'he'll live for ever.'"

The merchant gasped.

"But magic is not for me," the stranger went on, shaking his head. "I was afraid. I ran away as fast as I could. Luckily, I soon stumbled on the path leading out of the forest, and here I am, more dead than alive, and very grateful for this delicious supper."

"A garment woven from this cloth can make a man live for ever?" the merchant asked eagerly, his eyes glowing as brightly as the strange bird's wings. "But this cottage, and the fairy – surely they were only a dream?"

"No, no," the stranger insisted, and drawn out by the merchant's subtle questions he described exactly where the forest lay, and the place where he had entered it.

The very next morning, as soon as the stranger had gone, the merchant began to prepare for a journey of his own.

"Where are you going, Father?" his son asked anxiously.

"To find the magic cloth that will make me live for ever," his father said, and though his son pleaded with him to stay, he would not listen, but saddled his horse and rode away, kicking up the dust behind him in his haste.

Week after week, month after month, the merchant's son waited and hoped for his father's return. Every morning he scanned the horizon, and every evening he lit a lamp and set it by the door. But his father never came home.

At last, filled with foreboding, he set out to search for him. After long days and sleepless nights, he came to the deep forest. He plunged into it, but the path soon disappeared and he found himself lost and quite alone. Great trees rose up all around him, while on the ground thorns and fallen logs lay

in his way. Scratched and exhausted, he struggled on, drinking from forest pools to quench his thirst, with nothing but a few wild berries to eat.

When he was almost ready to give up and die, he stumbled into a clearing, and there, in the middle of it, was a cottage. A young woman with long white hair appeared at the door.

"Who are you?" she called out. "And what do you want?"

The young man's heart was beating fast, but the fairy was so pretty and gentle that he could not be afraid.

"I'm searching for my father, who came to find you. He wanted to ask you for the cloth that would make him live for ever," he tried to tell her, but he was so tired and faint with hunger that he staggered and nearly fell.

The fairy led him into her cottage and set in front of him a delicious meal. The merchant's son fell on it ravenously, and while he ate, he watched in wonder as the forest animals served their mistress. A lynx with yellow eyes was quietly grinding wheat on a grindstone, a shaggy bear was making bread, while a sleek otter was laying out to dry the clothes he had washed in the stream.

Night soon came, and the young man lay down on the bed of furs which the fairy provided for him and fell fast asleep, lulled by the clack of the loom where she sat and wove her hair.

He woke with a start at the sound of voices. A little man no higher than his knee, with a cap of leaves, shoes of nutshells and a coat made of bark, had entered the fairy's cottage.

"Tell me the news," the fairy commanded, as her shuttle flew backwards and forwards.

"Nothing to tell," said the elf. "All's quiet in the forest today."

A huge frog hopped up beside him.

"*Gra, graa*," croaked the frog. "I ain't seen nothing neither."

A great fox appeared.

"Nothing to report, dear mistress," he panted, flopping down at the fairy's feet.

And then, while the merchant's son watched in wonder, a fiery glow shone outside the open door. It grew brighter and brighter as into the cottage flew a bird, his feathers as brilliant as the sun.

"And what have you seen, golden bird?" asked the fairy, putting down her shuttle to stroke his dazzling head.

"I saw nothing," said the bird, "but I heard the jays squawking to each other. They've seen an old man captured by the jinns, who have made him their slave. The man was bent over, ploughing a field for his wicked masters. There were no horses or oxen to pull the plough, only a pair of deer. The man looked so worn and sad that even those silly jays wept at the sight of him."

"*Gra-graa*," croaked the frog. "He's a fool. Why don't he run away?"

"The jinns have taken his memory from him," answered the bird. "He's forgotten his home, his family and even his own name."

In his dark corner, the merchant's son lay listening intently, his heart full of pity and horror.

"Father! It must be Father!" he whispered to himself. "Oh, what can I do to help him?"

It was as if the fairy had read his thoughts.

"Can anything be done to save this poor man?" she asked the golden bird.

The bird nodded, and the glowing feathers of his crest brushed against the fairy's loom.

"There is a way," he said. "A young man could save him – but who would dare go near the jinns and risk being caught?"

"I would! Oh, I would!" thought the merchant's son.

"And he would need help from your magic too," the bird went on.

"My magic? How?" asked the fairy.

"He would have to take three twigs from the oak tree that grows above your cottage, and water from your well. At the moment when the sun goes down – no sooner and no later – he would have to hit the old man with the twigs and sprinkle him with the water. Only then would his memory return."

The merchant's son nearly cried out with excitement, but he stopped himself just in time.

"I'll do it! I'll set out tomorrow," he told himself. Then he closed his eyes and fell into a deep sleep.

The next morning, he told the fairy that he had heard the golden bird's story.

"That poor man's my father. I'm sure of it," he said.

"Go and find him, then," she said at once. "Take twigs from my tree, and water from my well. The fox will come with you to help you."

She snapped her fingers, and the fox trotted up.

"Climb on his back," she told the young man, "and your journey will be over before you know it."

So the merchant's son climbed on to the fox's back, who raced off with such speed that when they rushed through the forest, the leaves on the trees shivered as if a storm wind was blowing through them.

The sun was still high in the sky when they came to the edge of a field, and there, his back bent low, his poor muscles straining, was the merchant. He was shouting in a hoarse, cracked voice at the deer pulling the plough.

Quite forgetting the danger from the jinns and the instructions of the golden bird, his son ran towards him.

"Father! Father! I've found you at last!" he cried.

His father looked at him briefly and turned away. There was no recognition in his eyes.

"Get on, you lazy beasts!" he shouted, raising his whip to strike the deer.

The young man's eyes filled with tears. He tried to catch hold of his father's sleeve.

"Look at me, Father. You must know me. I'm your son!"

But his father only raised the whip again, threatening to bring it down with a crack on the young man's head.

"Get away from me," he growled. "Can't a man get on with his work in peace? Don't you know how my masters will punish me if this field isn't ploughed before the sun goes down?"

His son remembered the golden bird's words.

"Of course! I must wait till sunset," he told himself, "and I'd better hide, in case the jinns come out and catch me."

He slipped back to the shelter of the forest and, as the hot afternoon passed, he watched sorrowfully as his father struggled to plough the field.

At last the great red ball of the sun touched the horizon and began to sink. The merchant's son ran forward, struck his father with the oak twigs and emptied the bottle of fairy water over his head.

The sky went black and a wind howled, churning up the dust of the ploughed field so that it spiralled in twisty pillars right up to the sky.

When at last all was calm again, the moon shone out serenely. And as the young man stared into his father's face, he saw love and joy and memory return.

"Oh my boy, my dear, dear son," the merchant said. "What a fool I've been! And I was wicked, too. I would have stolen the fairy's magic cloth if she had refused to give it to me. I wanted to live for ever, but instead I became a mindless slave."

The fox, waiting at the forest fringe, gave a warning bark.

"Father, we must go," the merchant's son said urgently. "The jinns might come out at any moment and catch us."

Riding on the fox's back, the two of them journeyed through the night, and when dawn came they reached the fairy's clearing.

They ran to the cottage, eager to thank the fairy for all she had done. But the door was swinging in the breeze, and no light shone from within. The merchant and his son stepped inside. The cottage was empty. The fire on the hearth was out, and the loom was silent and still.

"Where is she? Where has she gone?" the merchant cried.

The bear, the lynx and the otter crept out of the forest and clustered sadly by the open door.

"She's gone! She's left us!" said the bear.

"Gone! Gone!" echoed the otter.

"The spirits of eternal life came, and took her from us," the lynx said, blinking tears from her yellow eyes. "They were afraid that a human would steal her cloth and live for ever, and that should never be."

The merchant and his son set out at once for home, and when they arrived safe and sound, they gave a great feast to celebrate their return.

"I've learned my lesson," the merchant told his friends. "I don't fear old age any longer, and when death comes to me I'll welcome him as a friend."

He lived contentedly for many more years, and when death did come, it was not the end, for he survived a long, long time in the memory of all those who loved and honoured him.

Acknowledgements

The stories in this book have been adapted from various sources including:

Persian Tales, D.L.R. and E.O'Lorimer (privately printed, 1919).

Persian Folk and Fairy Tales, retold by Anne Sinclair Mehdevi (Chatto and Windus, 1966).

Persian Fairy Tales, Jaroslav Tichy, retold by Jane Carruth (Hamlyn, 1970).

Folk Tales from Persia, Alan S. Feinstein (A.S.Barnes and Co., 1971).